# Three Little Doves

Taila Cantrell

# Contents

# Dedication

This is for my thick ladies. Let your freak flag fly baby, the ones for you will want you no matter what.
And for Leah. You have been such a huge part of my author journey. It's an honor to be your best friend.

# Trigger Warnings

Attempted Murder
Light Stalking
Mentions of Child Abuse
Forced Orgasms
MFFM
Dubious Consent
Murder/Death
Knife Play

# One

I liked my job. I really did. The Hex Guard paid well, had fantastic benefits, and I got to occasionally help witches in need. Today, though… today I hated being an assassin. Here's the thing about my line of work. You didn't just swing into buildings and slit people's throats. You had to follow them, gather intel, and be certain that the reports made against them were true. I had been trying to substantiate the claims made against Markus Withersby, Priest of the Black Coven, since November. I'd found very little evidence of the accusations we received from an anonymous member of his coven, but the higher-ups were antsy for some reason.

I lay on my belly in the attic of his home, staring down through the slats that were in his bedroom. Sweat trickled down my forehead, dripping off the tip of my nose. In February, it shouldn't be this hot, but apparently, Markus kept his home unbearable year-round. Thank the Mother I wouldn't still be here at the end of this week.

"Take a deep breath," Markus instructed the human who was sprawled out naked on the bed before him. My Other sight showed me the pale pink of his magic as it coated the human; even from here, I could feel the sex magic. I was forced to ignore the heartbeat that pulsed in my core as I continued to watch the scene unfold. His magic was strong; I hadn't had sex in well over two years, so I was unsurprised by the effect it was having on me. I might have to go to the club I'd seen Markus attend a few nights before to blow off some steam. I didn't enjoy lying with humans, and the risk of sleeping with other witches was high. My position within the Hex Guard would end if I found my witch bond. I didn't necessarily agree with the rule, but if there was one thing I'd learned in my time as a Guard... You didn't argue with the rules the Hex Guard had in place. It wasn't worth making your life that difficult.

I'd been a ward of the Hex Guard since I was eleven. Of course, I hadn't been born into it. Originally, I was part of the Dovey Coven in the mountains of Tennessee. When Garith came to raid the coven,  he'd decided to take me in. There had been so much blood... So many of my relatives dead that night... Garith was ruthless when he was given a task. The fact that he'd saved me was true mercy. I learned not to ask why the Dovey Coven had been targeted.

A shout of pleasure returned my mind to the scene occurring in the room underneath me. I looked down just as Markus threw his head back in pleasure, the muscles in his back and shoulders convulsing. There was no denying just how attractive this man was. His dark blonde hair was styled in a roughish way, curling around his ears and the nape of his neck. His skin was perfectly tan and unblemished. He would never look twice in my direction. I knew his type all too well. My curvaceous body had been a help many times when I was stalking my targets. Most extremely attractive people didn't pay attention to those of us they deemed below them. Any insecurity I'd had about my rolls and curves had been beaten out of me while I was training for the Guard. All that mattered was the mission. At least according to my superiors.

"That was lovely, darling. I'll have someone escort you home shortly." Markus told the girl as he assisted her in sitting up. It was clear that she was in a daze, but no true harm had been done. He sat with her for a long moment while she caught her breath, handing her clothes and supplies to shower before she left. Once she was on her feet and had her wits about her, Markus disappeared from the room.

I sighed, knowing that I'd have to crawl around the attic until I found him again. At least this assignment would be over soon enough; maybe I would request a short leave once I'd taken care of Markus. I could use a weekend on a private beach with nothing but a strong drink and a smut novel.

# Two

I cursed as I tripped over the curb, nearly face-planting in the small heels I'd forced myself to wear. Unfortunately, I couldn't stay in my comfy black athletic wear I usually wore. Rubies was filled with other witches, and I would stand out if I didn't dress more like everyone else. I didn't really want to be here, but I'd overheard a conversation between some of the staff at Markus' home that he and some other woman would be here tonight. A club was a good place to lure someone away. I doubted seduction would work, but I'd find a way.

"Are you okay, red?" A melodic voice asked from behind me. I turned to find a striking  woman. My eyes went to her  hair first, half was dyed pitch black while the other half was platinum blonde. It fell to her shoulders in perfect waves.  She was absolutely stunning. Her greyish blue eyes held humor as I struggled to respond. I switched to my Other sight to learn that she was a sex witch. A pink crown lay over her brow, denoting her status within the coven. "I'm Alura. You must be new around here."

I gathered myself, "Yes. I'm Xava Dovey, just visiting."

"You're not used to dressing like this." She pointed out.

I snorted, "Guilty. This isn't my usual scene."

"Well, follow me, red. I'll introduce you to some of the best people in town." She said, offering me her arm.

"You sound like the wolf about to gobble me up," I responded without thinking.

Her laugh caressed my skin, "I like you, Xava. Might have to convince you to stick around for a while."

Considering that she was one of Markus' coven members, I doubted I'd stick around her for too long, but maybe I could use her to get close to him. The Hex Guard may not care, but I'd like to be a little more certain before I took the man's life.

"I never stay in one place for long," I responded, allowing her to drag me into the Rubies club. Magic was thick in the air, and my desire to wrap a shield around myself pounded in the back of my head. I'd been trained never to have my back to a witch that I didn't know, much less hundreds of them.

"How does your coven feel about that?" Alura asked, eyeing me in a way that made me feel naked. She was very perceptive, which only doubled her attractiveness to me.

"We're all nomadic," I responded. It wasn't technically untrue. To outsiders, I was a covened witch, but in reality, there was no coven within the Hex Guard. We were bound by our oaths. It wasn't impossible to leave, just highly discouraged.

"That must be lonely." She responded as she made her way through the crowd. Everyone moved out of her way as she almost floated through the room. Alura was... aptly named. As if her parents had taken one look at her and known that she would be able to lure anyone to her side.

"It can be," I said, honestly.

Alura led me up some stairs, opening a door and letting me enter first. The room was darker than the rest of the club; only red lights lit the room. "Markus, I've brought a guest," Alura announced as she moved deeper into the room.

"A play toy or friend." A male voice asked.

I raised an eyebrow as Markus came into view. His blonde hair was perfectly coiffed, and silver rimmed glasses sat on his straight nose, giving him an academic air. I'd never seen him wear them before, but I forced myself not to ask. To them, I was a pitiful stranger, not an assassin who had been stalking them for weeks. Markus' green eyes landed on me, a smile curled up his lips, "A playful friend, I hope." His eyes roamed down my body, giving me pause. I wasn't expecting the lust in his eyes as he crossed the room to press a kiss into my offered hand. "Markus Withersby, Priest of the Black Coven. What's your name, beautiful?"

"Lay off it, Markus. This is Xava, and I highly doubt she's interested in your pretentious compliments." Alura said, laying a hand on his shoulder.

"I didn't realize you'd already laid claim, Priestess." He said, smiling at me before he turned toward her, "How is my lovely bond this evening?"

They were bonded? I switched to my Other sight, finding a purple cord that connected them at the pinky. It was lighter than any I'd seen before, almost as if the bond was strained. Alura was the Priestess of the Black Coven. If I did follow the command of the Hex Guard, I'd be killing her, too. Witch bonds couldn't live without each other; something about the way their magics mingled made it impossible for the other person to live. Of course, a witch didn't die first; they lost their sanity. I'd been called in on two assassinations for warlocks that had lost their bond. It was the most heartbreaking thing I'd ever witnessed.

"Xava, you there?" Alura asked.

"Ah, sorry. Lost in thought." I said, heat climbing up my cheeks.

"Markus asked where you're from... originally." She said, "Come sit and chat with us."

Somehow, I ended up seated between Markus and Alura on a large leather couch. None of us were touching, but I could still feel the heat of their bodies. Once again, the pounding between my legs started. These sex witches were dangerous. "Tennessee," I said once we'd settled.

"I've been to the Smokies several times. It's a beautiful place." Markus purred, "Almost as beautiful as you."

Alura rolled her eyes at his flirtation, "He can't help himself around a beautiful witch."

"Neither can Alura. Don't let her fool you, she doesn't bring just anyone into our box." He said.

"Your box?" I asked, interested in learning more about them.

"Oh yes, I am a partial owner in Rubies. They created this space just for me." He explained, "I assisted in ensuring that none of their patrons would be sexually preyed upon. There's a spell in place that discourages groping and harassment."

"That's impressive," I responded. It sounded more like a Protection spell than a sexual one. While witches could do some magic that didn't fall into their particular designation, it wasn't an easy thing to learn.

"I dabble with many different forms of magic," He smirked, "But that's enough about me. Tell us how you ended up here."

I hesitated, but wove a story that was made of partial truths and plenty of lies. As we spoke, I found myself relaxing and enjoying their company. Markus was flirtatious, but not disrespectful. Alura was more reserved, but whenever she did interject, it was witty. My instincts screamed that the accusations made against Markus were false, but I had no idea how to handle Garith if I didn't follow orders.

When I glanced down at my watch and found that it was three am, I stood, "I have to get back to my hotel. It's been a pleasure talking to both of you this evening."

"Please come see us again," Markus said, pressing another kiss to the back of my hand. His warm lips lingered for a long moment, green eyes staring into mine.

"I will if I can before I leave," I responded, noncommittally.

Alura stood, smoothing her dress before she reached out, wrapping me in a hug. The smell of her perfume was heady, and I couldn't stop myself from hugging her back. "I've enjoyed your company, Xava. Please visit me again."

I nodded before showing myself out of the room. The music of the club was a surprise as I closed the door behind me. I rushed out of there like a demon was on my heels. When I got to my car, I finally took a deep breath. How was I going to kill Markus, and by default, Alura? They'd shown no sign of breaking any laws, much less being predatory. I decided to head back to my hotel. I was going to have to contact Garith. Whether I wanted to or not.

It took me two hours to convince myself to pick up the phone. It had been a mistake. I held my head in my hands as Garith continued to drone on about duty. "Just because you haven't seen the behavior doesn't mean it hasn't happened. We've received a report--"

"What's the point of my spending three months here watching them if my recommendation isn't going to be respected?" I snapped.

The line was silent for a long moment, and dread built in my chest. "I'm going to send someone out there."

"That's not nec--" Before I could finish my sentence, the line went dead.

Anxiety kept me sitting there staring at my black phone for a long, long time. Who would Garith send?

# Three

At least today I wasn't trapped in an attic watching Markus work his magic on another human. I'd slept too late, catching Markus just as he was leaving his home. I'd managed to keep up in my car, watching from a distance as he picked up Alura. It was strange to me that they didn't live together, considering that they were bonded. I hadn't even seen Alura until last night. Only catching wind of the Priestess a few times during the time that I'd been watching Markus. I grew even more curious as they drove for over an hour, winding up at a tiny cabin. I parked down the road, marching through the cold wind and trees to the cabin that they were already settled inside of. I muttered a spell, allowing myself to fade through the back door unseen. I realized too late that there was no attic in the small space, so I worked a second spell, cloaking myself so that I could listen to them from nearby. This wasn't ideal. If I grew tired or I was sensed by one of them, my cover would be blown, but I had to know what was going on here.

"I hate doing this." Alura's voice was harsh as she spoke.

"Me too, but until we have a better option, it's all we can do," Markus responded. There were sounds of shuffling, and I faded myself into the bedroom.

"Why would the Mother curse us to this?" She growled back. She was completely nude, her perky breasts bouncing slightly as she crossed her arms.

"I don't know, Lura. I am sorry, you know that." He said, laying his pants carefully to the side.

I couldn't prepare myself for the burst of pink magic that he suddenly tossed at Alura. My instincts kicked in, my magic responding to my emotions more than anything. A shimmering shield stopped the blast just before it made contact with Alura. Both of them stumbled backward before their eyes turned toward me. A dark purple light burst from where our magics met, slamming into all three of us. Markus shouted just before I passed out.

I came back into consciousness swinging. Markus wasn't prepared for the punch that landed in his sternum. He yelped, rushing backward. "What the fuck." I said, reaching for the knife concealed at my back.

"Xava, it's okay. I'm not really sure why you're here, but sit down so we can discuss this calmly." Alura's voice was strained as she took me in.

"Are you okay?" I asked seriously, stepping toward her before stopping myself.

"I'm fine. What... What are you doing here? Do you know what just happened?"

The questions made my brain hurt, but the strange pounding in my chest had me sitting down. "Oh no. No no no no no."

"Whoa, it's okay, Xava. Just take a deep breath." Markus said, sitting next to me, "The witch bond can be very intense in the early stages. We have plenty of time to discuss how to handle this."

My eyes widened as he spoke my worst fear, "We need to get out of this state."

They both recoiled at my statement, but Alura asked, "Why? What's going on?"

My chest constricted as panic filled my body. I'd never felt this way before; my breathing became rapid. A warm hand on the back of my neck shocked me. I cut my eyes to Markus pressed down on my neck, "Trust me." I allowed him to fold my body forward, my forehead nearly touching my knees. "Breathe in through your nose and out through your mouth." I followed his instructions, slowly he let me sit up, but kept his hand on my neck, lightly massaging as we breathed in sync. My heartbeat slowed down, and I slowly returned to my normal self. "Are you feeling normal again?"

I nodded, "I apologize. That's never happened to me before."

"Don't apologize for having a panic attack. Clearly, there's something wrong. Can you let us in on why we need to leave the state?" Alura chimed in.

I took one last deep breath before I began to speak, "I'm sorry for everything I'm about to tell you. You have to understand that the oaths I've taken bind me in ways that Coven oaths don't." I paused, but neither of them responded, nodding for me to continue. "I am sworn to the assassin division of the Hex Guard." The news rippled through the room. Alura leaned back, her face becoming pale. While Markus just stared at me, eyes narrowing. When no one rushed to say anything, I continued, "I know very well how most people feel about the role I was given within the Hex Guard. I want to be clear that this was not the life I chose for myself, but the Hex Guard can be very convincing." I trailed off, waiting for them to attack me. When their silence continued, I went on. "I was sent here to assess Markus in November due to allegations that were made anonymously about his treatment of humans and his coven."

"And what did you determine?" Markus interrupted.

"I witnessed no behaviors that are against any law... However, my boss insisted that I proceed with the execution." I responded.

"Is that what you were here to do?" Alura asked quietly.

I was quiet for a long moment, "I came here to... I don't know how to explain this. I just felt like I needed to understand more about your relationship. No one had explained to me that a witch bond was at play here." Alura stood, pacing the room as I continued. "I tried to explain to my commander that I hadn't witnessed even a hint of any of what had been accused. When I insisted that I wouldn't move forward with an execution... He told me he would send someone else here."

"So there is another assassin coming to end my life... and now by extension both of yours," Markus said. "Is any of what you told us true? Is your name even Xava?"

"Xava Dovey is my real name... I think we should figure out a plan of action before we try to dive into my life story." I responded.

"Who could have made a report to the Hex Guard?" Alura asked, suddenly. "To report that you were breaking those laws, someone would have to be in the Coven."

Markus sat back, staring up at the ceiling for a long moment. "We both know the only person who has a problem with me in the coven."

"He wouldn't," Alura said.

"Who?" I hadn't paid much attention to the members of Markus' coven; clearly, that had been a mistake.

"He's been mad ever since Fang left to join Blood. Says that I allowed the coven to be weakened." Markus ignored my question as he spoke to Alura.

"He found his bond! What were you supposed to do?" She ranted, "I'll have his head on a sspike if we prove that he did this."

Without thinking, I said, "Killing a member of your own coven is one of the fastest ways to bring the Hex Guard down on you."

They stared at me, before Markus said, "I guess you would know. What do you suggest that we do?"

"First, we need to find out if this person you're thinking of did make the report. If it was done out of vengeance, and I can prove that we won't have a problem." I said, "Second, we'll need to discuss this problem between us. Why did you attack Alura?"

Markus and Alura glanced at each other, having a conversation with their eyes that I couldn't read. Finally, Alura sighed, "He wasn't attacking me. I'm... I'm a lesbian, Xava. Our bond and place within the coven requires that we sleep together at times. When we must do so without a female buffer, Markus uses his magic to... assist."

"I make sure it's still pleasurable for her." Markus added, "The man who I think made the report is Vince Parth. Had Fang and I not joined the Black Coven, he would have been the next Priest. He's never liked me, but after Fang left, it's been much more apparent."

"We can't leave our coven behind, Xava. Not to even mention that we have a major ritual coming up on the fourteenth. We'll just have to hope that the Mother and Father are on our side." Alura said, "We stay here tonight, and discuss what we need to do."

My gut twisted at her words. I knew staying here was a bad idea, but I could see in her eyes that there was no chance that she was going to change her mind. Markus agreed as he said, "Yes, the bond is the more important thing to deal with right now."

"More important than your possible execution?" I argued.

"Are you planning to execute me?" He shot back.

"Of course not! It's just..." I sighed, trailing off. I didn't want to see either one of them harmed when I could prevent it. Staying here was a mistake; if we left and regrouped, I could plan a way to bring this to Garith and the rest of the commanders in the Hex Guard.

They would have to see reason. Denying a witch their bond was against the laws of the Mother and Father. "I interrupted a spell you needed to perform. Why don't y'all finish that up?" I changed the subject, unable to put all of my thoughts into words.

Alura and Markus looked at each other before he said, "You can say no to what I'm about to suggest... Would you join us in completing the spell? It would save Alura a lot of anguish if she didn't have to sleep with me."

"What spell did I stop you from using earlier?" I asked instead of answering his question.

"It makes me perceive Markus as a woman for a short period of time. Something we created shortly after the bond formed, and we realized that not sleeping together wasn't an option." Alura explained.

"That's... genius," I said, before I began chewing on my lip. For weeks, I'd watched Markus sleep with a variety of women, never considering that I'd have the opportunity for myself. I wasn't nearly as experienced as either of them; I'd likely be a disappointment.

"It's okay to say no. We'll go at your pace." Alura said, "The spell works just fine. I can handle it one more time."

"I'll do it," I said, straightening my spine. "If the Mother and Father have bound the three of us, I have a duty to you."

"You take your duties very seriously, don't you?" Markus mused as he stood. "Hopefully, we'll show you that sex is not about duty." He held out his hand, so I took it, allowing him to lead Alura and I back to the bedroom.

Alura had no hesitation is stripping out of the simple black leggings and t shirt that she wore. I appreciated the curves of her body as she stepped toward me, gripping the bottom of my long-sleeved shirt, her steel blue eyes staring into mine. "I wanted you in my bed the moment I saw you trip on the curb at Rubies. I couldn't be happier that the Hex Guard sent you here." She said as she removed my top.

"If only she weren't here to murder me," Markus said, pulling my attention to him. He stood, completely nude, watching us. I couldn't keep my eyes from drifting down to his cock. It stood at attention, curving toward his stomach. I looked away quickly. Markus sighed, "You don't prefer men."

"No, no... I'm bisexual. It's just... I've never been with anyone... your size." Heat rushed to my cheeks as I admitted that. I wasn't experienced in bed; the few encounters I'd had were rushed, fumbling attempts. "I've never... finished."

Alura grabbed my face, pulling my attention to her, "That changes now. Let us take care of you." With that, Alura and Markus surrounded me, both of them running hands over my body, exploring me in a way I'd never been explored before. The rest of my clothes were yanked off me and tossed haphazardly out of the way. When Alura bent her head, sucking one of my nipples into her mouth, I nearly screamed from the pleasure. "So very sensitive." She looked at Markus over my shoulder, "The Mother and Father have truly blessed us."

"I only dreamed that we'd be here when we talked in the club last night." Markus said, "Xava, you are gorgeous. These curves are to die for." Alura continued to play with my nipples, but when a hand cupped my throbbing pussy I felt a zip of pleasure run down my spine. These two had me so close to the edge without hardly any effort; there was no way I could keep up with them in bed. A thick finger slipped inside me, "Al, position?"

Alura pulled away, "Would you like to eat my pussy while Markus fucks you?"

My eyes widened at the thought as I nodded my head frantically. Alura grinned, crawling onto the bed and spreading her legs. Her pussy was completely bald, making me slightly nervous about the manicured landing strip I maintained. "Come here, pet." I scrambled onto the bed at her instruction. I pressed my lips to her thigh, slowly making my way to her pussy. I'd done this before, so I felt confident as I delved into her sweet scent. Her fingers tangled into my hair just as I felt Markus climb onto the bed behind me.

"Father, this ass may be the death of me." He said, his hands palming my ass cheeks, spreading them. "Soon Alura will take one of your holes with her strap, while I take your ass." The words rang through my head, conjuring images that flooded my pussy with heat. "So wet and ready for me."

"Hurry the fuck up. She's good at this." Alura groaned as I sucked her clit. Markus didn't need any more prompting; his cock pressed into me gently, filling me in a way that I'd never been filled before. I forced myself to focus on Alura's pleasure instead of the intense feeling as he bottomed out. I sucked and licked in time with Markus' strokes, until her nails dug into my shoulder and I felt the muscles in her thighs begin to shake. Markus began chanting words that I could barely make out over the feelings that flooded me. Magic was thick in the air as Alura screamed out her release. I continued to lap at her until she pulled away.

Markus grabbed my hair, pulling me up so my breasts bounced in Alura's face as he fucked me harder, still chanting. How he could fuck and work magic at the same time was a mystery to me.

"Look at you, taking his big cock so well. Do you love the way it feels inside you?" Alura asked, palming both of my breasts.

I nodded, unable to form words. Markus panted as his hips continued to snap into mine, "Make her cum."

Alura didn't hesitate, her hands running down the curve of my belly until she found the sensitive bud. Her lips met mine, her honey and strawberry taste overwhelming my senses as she kissed me. I ground into her fingers, feeling so close to the edge. Markus' fingers dug into my hips, slamming harder into me once... twice... three times before I saw stars. A scream ripped from me as my orgasm flooded through my body. Markus pulled out, and I felt the spray of his cum as it coated my ass. We all collapsed onto the bed, panting.

"That. Was. Amazing." I said, unable to help the smile on my face.

"Just wait until we introduce you to more. I have a toy closet that any sex addict would admire." Alura said, "I assume you don't know much about BDSM?"

"I... I've seen a few things I'd be interested in trying." I admitted, unable to stop the embarrassment that welled up inside me.

"It's okay that you aren't as experienced as we are," Markus said, "In fact, introducing you to our world is a pleasure."

"I like bondage. The idea of being tied up is appealing, but I'd also like to try tying someone else up." I said.

"I don't enjoy being submissive, but Alura is a switch." He said.

"A switch?" I asked, glancing at her.

"A switch is someone who enjoys being dominant or submissive. Markus only enjoys being dominant." She explained.

"Oh... I'm a switch, I think."

"Let's rest. That spell took a lot out of me. We have plenty of time to explore your kinks." Markus said, standing from the bed. "I do like you covered in my cum, but why don't we get you cleaned up?"

I nodded, allowing him to wipe me down with wipes he produced from the nightstand. Alura handed me my clothes, but I chose to only throw on my t-shirt and panties before climbing in between them on the bed.

"I know the circumstances we've met under aren't ideal, but I'm very excited to know more about you, Xava. I hope you'll feel the same after this business with the Hex Guard is over." Markus said, tossing an arm around my waist.

As I drifted off to sleep, I said, "This is the happiest I've been in many, many years."

# Four

We spent another day in the remote cabin, talking and learning each other in a way I'd never had with anyone else before. Relationships were superficial at best in the Hex Guard, while there were some partnerships and teams, most of the work we did was solo. At least in the assassin division. I didn't know as much about the operations of the rest of Hex Guard.

"So you started in the Hex Guard when you were thirteen?" Alura asked as she pulled her hair into a ponytail. For the first time, I noticed the tattoo that was hidden underneath her hair on the back of her head, stretching down her neck. I couldn't stop myself from running my fingers over the swirling ink. She groaned, "That's one way to avoid answering a question."

"Oh... sorry." I muttered, pulling away, "Yes, Garith gave me two years to adjust to being in the Hex Guard. He is head of the assassin division, so there was no other choice for where I'd go."

"It's okay to touch me," She said, grabbing my hand, "My neck is just a very sensitive part of my body."

"How did you stand to get it tattooed?" I asked, appreciating that she dropped the subject of my brutal teen years.

"I did it." Markus chimed in as he exited the shower.

I watched as the water droplets traced down his golden skin, "You tattoo?" I finally asked.

"Occasionally. My duties as a Priest make it hard to do anything full-time." He explained, stepping into the closet to dress.

My brain returned to normal when all of his perfect muscles weren't taunting me. The witch bond must have flipped a switch in me that I didn't know existed. I could live on Markus' perfectly cut cock, imagining him tattooing Alura did something to me that I couldn't even begin to explain. I wanted to ask him to put his ink on me as well. It was too soon. I shook my head, distracting myself with a spell to summon some of my clothes. I hadn't intended to stay the night here, much less spend the majority of my time naked. My body was the most relaxed it had ever been, and as I slipped into the brown pants and white t-shirt that had appeared for me, I took the deepest breath of my life. For the first time since I was eleven years old I had a family. It might still be new, but I knew that Alura and Markus would care for me regardless of all the blood that stained my hands.

"You can ride back with us. I'd love to introduce you to the coven." Markus offered.

I shook my head, "That isn't a good plan. Not yet. My car is just downhill. I'll come see y'all later on."

His brows furrowed together, "I don't like that plan. We shouldn't be separated so early into our bond."

"I've been taking care of myself for a very long time. I promise I'll be okay." I said, laying a hand over his heart. It beat in rhythm with mine, surprising me. Just how deep did the bond the Mother and Father blessed us with go? I needed to do more research. I'd never taken the time to learn more about witch bonds; it seemed unnecessary.

He sighed, "You're used to being alone, but you aren't anymore. It's fine... this time."

I quirked a brow, "You're not the boss of me."

His green eyes darkened, and he gripped my hand, pulling me closer, "You won't find that I take well to bratty behavior, Xava. I'd hate to have to introduce you to edging when you've had so few orgasms."

"Edging?" I asked, ignoring the huskiness of my voice.

"He'll bring you to the edge of orgasm, but not let you finish. Over and over again." Alura explained.

"Oh... no, I don't want that," I whined, but the idea of that level of control did something to my insides,

"Then be a good girl." Markus winked at me, returning to his usual chipper attitude as he shouldered their bags.

They dropped me off at my car, and I watched until they were out of my sight. My heart squeezed slightly, but I forced myself to dig my cell phone out of the glovebox and turn it back on. I gulped when I saw the large number of missed calls from Garith. Instead of calling him, I turned my phone back off, started my car, and drove back into town.

I slipped into my hotel room, sighing as I glanced at my suitcase open on the bed. I understood that Markus and Alura had to stay in town, especially with the upcoming holiday, but I knew that at any moment that we may need to run. I took a long time to refold my clothes and items and carefully place them back into my bag. When I finished, I sat on the bed, staring at the walls. It was hard to believe that I'd found not just one but two bonds. It changed everything about my life. I just didn't know how to tell the Hex Guard that I'd be leaving. I was one of the top assassins in the county. There had been whispers for years that I would take

Garith's place. No one had ever asked me if that was something I was interested in. Of course, I wasn't. What I wanted most in the world was to go home. To the rolling hills of Tennessee. I hadn't been allowed the set foot back in the state since I'd been ripped away from my parents. The mountains called me, but I'd never been allowed to answer. Maybe I could convince Alura and Markus to visit soon.

"You're a hard woman to find." Magic burst out of me as a male voice interrupted my musings.

I twirled around, a sword made of my magic instantly forming in my hand as a golden shield wrapped around my body. When I saw Dagger Ladron standing in the corner of the room, I froze. "What are you doing here?"

"Garith sent me to check on you." He responded, pushing his black hair out of his eyes. His strange, pale eyes pinned me to the spot as he moved toward me. "You've got a secret."

My eyes widened, "I don't know what you're talking about."

"Oh, so the purple flecks in your aura aren't your witch bond?" He shot back.

"Please… Dagger…" I made my sword vanish. "We were friends once."

He hummed as he circled me, "That was a long time ago, Xava. Before you refused to work with me anymore." He reached out to touch me, but my shield remained in place, and his hand bounced away. He laughed darkly, "Garith won't be happy that you've hidden this from him. His perfect little daughter, bonding without permission."

"No witch can stand between bound witches." I shot back.

"Mhm, maybe when you're a free witch, but you've sworn oaths." Dagger pointed out. "Surely you can think of a way to convince me to keep this little secret."

Something about the way he said it... Dagger was a death warlock; he'd joined the Hex Guard when he was seventeen. I'd heard a rumor that the coven he'd been from was eradicated due to practicing cannibalism. What could he possibly want from me? "I could always just tell Garith myself." I pointed out.

"If you wanted to do that, you would have already." He said, "Drop your shield, let's chat."

"How do I know you won't attack me?" I asked wearily.

"For old time's sake, Xava. Just two old friends catching up." He held up his hands, taking a seat in a chair. "I won't hurt you unless you ask for it."

My breath hitched against my will, my newly, easily aroused body clenching at the words. Markus and Alura had taught me a lot in the short time I'd spent with them, but something about the dark way that Dagger said that had me wanting to obey him. Slowly, I exhaled, dropping my shield and taking a seat on the edge of the bed. "Say what you want to say." I insisted.

He stared at me until I started to squirm, "Why did you refuse to work with me?" He finally asked, "And don't lie. I'll know if you're lying." I bit my cheek; I didn't want to tell him the truth. I hadn't even told Garith the truth when I'd requested to start working solo. "Time is ticking, cherry."

The sound of his nickname for me cut through the last of my defenses. "Fine... I requested to work solo because on that last mission... I was more worried about protecting you than I was ending the target."

"And why is that?" He leaned forward.

"I... I had feelings for you." I admitted. Before I could blink, Dagger was in my space, tangling a hand into my hair as his lips crashed into mine in a violent kiss. His grip on my hair was painful as he slipped his tongue into my mouth, the taste of coffee flooding my senses. I groaned, spreading my legs to give him more room. I couldn't even think as he devoured my mouth.

The sound of my hotel door smacking open finally forced me to push Dagger away. I couldn't process anything as Markus came flying into the room, his fist smacking into Dagger's face. "That's my fucking bond." He growled, aiming a kick at Dagger's balls.

I glanced toward the doorway to see Alura leaning on the doorframe, looking concerned. I wanted to speak to her, but when Markus stumbled backward from a blow to the ribs that Dagger had delivered, I realized the fight was more pressing.

"Stop, stop. Dagger is an old..." My words fell on deaf ears as the two men fought, destroying the coffee table in the center of the room.

I sighed, muttering a spell as the two of them circled each other. Just as I sent the spell out, Dagger launched an attack at Markus. When the two spells collided, all of us were thrown backward. Purple light flashed, and I screamed as I felt another snap in my chest.

"Well... fuck..." Alura was the first to stand, glancing between Dagger and I as she wiped blood from her forehead. "He's... bonded to us as well?"

Markus groaned, "Why the fuck does this keep happening to me?"

Dagger sat on the floor, staring down at his hands before raising those nearly white eyes to meet mine. "We've got a big fucking problem."

"Yeah, no shit." I snapped.

*Five*

"Y ou can't be serious." Markus echoed for the third time as we all sat around the hotel room, nursing our wounds.

Apparently, the reason that Markus and Alura had come looking for me is that they'd gotten home and found a letter from several coven members insisting that they join before the coven on Valentine's Day or step down from their roles as Priest and Priestess. It was a perfect solution, even if I had managed to scrub their image clean in the Hex Guard's eyes, refusing to perform a ceremony on the sacred day to the Mother and Father would have been enough to give the coven to right to force them out.

"How was I supposed to know I'd ended up bonded to your stupid ass?" Dagger snapped. "Xava, we've got to get the fuck out of here. Garith and his posse will be here anytime."

"He's hell bent on killing Markus." I said, "But I don't understand why. No laws have been broken."

"Does it even matter?" Dagger sighed. "We have a half-completed bond, the most powerful members of the Hex Guard on the way here, and someone in the Black coven aiming to take control by Valentine's Day."

"We should stay and fight." Markus growled, "This is my coven. I don't want to give it up to that ugly fuckass."

"Fuckass?" I mimed back. The room was silent for a moment before we all burst into laughter. The sound of their laughter warmed a part of my heart that I didn't know was cold. "Markus, I know that you don't want to consider this, but… We need to leave. Even if it's just temporary, we need to regroup, complete our bond. If our bond is complete, Garith can't interfere with us. It gives us the chance to gather evidence that you didn't do what you're being accused of."

Alura sighed, "She's right, Mar. We could go stay at my parents' villa in Colorado."

"No, anything connected to our names won't be safe," Dagger said.

My heart fluttered as an idea formed in my mind, "Do y'all trust me?"

Three sets of eyes turned to me as all three of them said, "Without a doubt." In unison.

"Markus, Alura, go to your homes, gather your absolute necessities. Meet us back here in one hour." I instructed.

"Oh, you taking control is kind of hot," Alura said, standing to follow my directions.

I winked at her before ushering them out of the door. When Dagger and I were alone again, I said, "Do you know where I plan to go?"

He nodded, "It's dangerous. It may not be the first place he looks, but he will consider it. He will see it as a direct affront to him."

Something inside of me steeled, "Then let him come. He won't catch me unprepared like he did my family."

<h1 style="text-align:center">Six</h1>

C ommitting treason probably shouldn't be the most freeing moment of my life. As Markus, Alura, and Dagger talked quietly, I drove. Speeding around curves as we crossed over the Tennessee State line. We drove for hours, all of them slept, but my knuckles were white on the steering wheel. A hum had begun in my bones as we zipped along back roads, closer and closer to the mountains that I had been born in. When we reached the six-hour mark, Markus insisted on taking over driving.

I curled into the passenger seat, forcing my eyes to drift closed. I was swept away into a dream in the next breath.

*I didn't recognize my surroundings, but the white dress I wore was oddly familiar. I floated along the ground, following the sounds of a commotion I couldn't see. I glanced down, noticing that my feet were covered in dirt. Mama wouldn't be happy about that. I furrowed my brow, wracking my brain for why this was so familiar to me. When a female scream echoed around me, I started to run toward the noise. It was ingrained in my bones as a Protection witch to help others.*

*I slid to a stop at the horrific scene. Three hulking men stood in the center of at least ten bodies. My father's head was held aloft by* the man in the center, "There are a few more in some of the cabins to the north. Go deal with them while I call for clean up."

My body shook as my instincts took over. Words I barely even understood the meaning of rushed from my lips as I hurled a spell at the only man left. He was caught off guard as my spell hit him, my body launching on his back after it. He stumbled, and I screamed out my grief. I saw the cloudy eyes of my mother and her best friends clutching each other even in death. Golden magic wrapped around my fists as I beat them against the man. Even when I was flipped over his back and slammed into the Earth, breath rushing out of my lungs, I didn't stop.

His massive hand wrapped around my throat, his voice echoing as he said, "You're a firecracker. A bit fat, but we can turn that into muscle."

I growled like an animal, rage and grief warring in my mind as he lifted me up, keeping a tight hand around my throat. "What's your name?" I spat in his eye, but he just laughed at my efforts. "Yes, you'll do well for my prodigy."

The final thing I saw before I blacked out again was one of the men returning, my oldest brother's limp body thrown over his shoulder.

*Markus*

I could barely keep my eyes on the road as Xava murmured in her sleep. For the first time, I understood how Fang had felt on Halloween Night as he watched Bambi from the corner of the room. I wished I could pick up the phone and call him. He was a powerful warlock, well on his way to becoming the next Priest of

Blood. He would have been an ardent supporter of my remaining the head of the Black Coven, but I couldn't risk Xava and Alura's safety. Xava had asked for trust, and so I had given it to her freely. Plus, Fang had a duty to Bambi. A duty I hadn't entirely understood until I'd sunk my cock into Xava. I loved Alura, but it wasn't the same. We were friends, best friends even. I trusted her at my back more than anyone else, but we didn't share the same connection that the curvy redhead had shown me in just a few hours.

"Keep your fucking eyes on the road." Dagger snapped from the backseat. I hadn't even known he was awake.

"You realize we're going to have to learn to like each other, right?" I said. The girls were asleep, so it was time for us to have a conversation. "I saw the way you manhandled her in the hotel room. She didn't consent to that."

He snorted, opening those nearly white eyes to look at me in the rearview mirror. "You're only mad because you wish she'd respond to you like she does to me. Xava may have a dominant streak, but she will bend until she breaks in my hands."

"If you break her, I will rip you limb from limb," I growled.

"Only in the ways we both know that you like." He responded. I glared at him, "Oh, please, don't act like you don't have dark fantasies. You're a fucking sex warlock. Xava on her knees, begging and crying in pain and pleasure, would get your rocks off faster than you want to admit." I bit my tongue, unable to think of a good response. Unfortunately, he was right. Just the image of Xava on her knees had my cock stiffening in my pants. I didn't dare adjust myself for fear that he would realize just how much what he'd said had affected me. "I'm never going to hurt her." He muttered, meeting my eyes again, "She's been my greatest obsession for the last seven years."

"What was she like?" I couldn't help myself, I wanted to know as much about my perfect little bond as I could.

"I was seventeen when I joined the Hex Guard, and she was fifteen at the time. Already, she was a favorite among the top commanders. They paired us up because of our ages. They couldn't send us into the field in the same way since we were Unascended, but we trained together." He paused, clearly falling into those memories, "We worked together for ten years, side by side almost every day. She was my only friend, and then one day she disappeared from my life. I'd catch glimpses of her at meetings occasionally, but she was always so careful to avoid me."

"How didn't you bond back then? Surely you did spells together." I wondered aloud.

"Hex Guard assassins aren't allowed to perform spells with their counterparts for that exact reason. They don't want to lose us to the Mother and Father." He answered with no emotion, "I may bend her, but trust that I'll never truly break her. She owns me whether she knows that or not."

We lapsed into silence as we continued to drive. The GPS dinged as we entered a small town, Mercy Valley, letting me know that we had nearly reached our destination. The sun was peaking up over the horizon when we reached the hotel that Xava had selected for us. When I went to shake her awake, her skin was on fire. "What the fuck."

Dagger pitched forward, snapping his fingers in her ear before he cursed under his breath. "A Dream witch has her."

"What?" I nearly shouted, drawing the eyes of the few people milling around outside the hotel.

Alura yawned, uncurling herself, "What's going on?"

"Everyone just shut up for a minute." Dagger snapped, pulling out his cell phone. He punched a few buttons before someone picked up. I could hear the muffled male voice on the other end complaining, "No.... Okay, well, I need your help... Friend of mine is trapped by a dream witch... uh huh.... No...." Dagger was silent as the man grumbled for a few minutes before he finally said, "Is that safe?" Whatever the man responded made Dagger's darker skin pale. He hung up the phone and looked to us, "Let's get her up to our room. We're going to have to try to do a protection spell."

"But none of us are Protection witches." Alura pointed out.

"We'd better hope that the Mother and Father have really blessed our bond then." He responded gravely.

Xava looked peaceful as she lay unconscious on the bed. Her long red hair was stark against the white pillows. I wanted nothing more than for her to wake up and look at me with those soulful brown eyes.

"Okay, I think I've got it," Dagger said as he re-entered the room. His arms were laden with black candles. It was rare for a witch or warlock to resort to true spell casting, as most of us could use our magic without the need for a direction. Unfortunately, we were going to be attempting a spell that none of us were qualified to do. "Stand on either side of the bed." He directed as he set candles up all around Xava's body. None of us cared if wax dripped onto the bed as he lit them, "Join hands and repeat after me." We did as he instructed, our voices becoming one. "Mother, we call on you. Father, we call on you. Bless us tonight with the power of our bonded." The candles flickered slightly, but remained lit, "Allow us to access her Protection magic. Grant us a way to protect her as she would protect us." Xava's body glowed suddenly, the flames licking higher as our voices raised. "*Mater, Pater, permitte nobis purgare magiam quae dilectam nostram infecit. Aufer ab ea maledictionem in mente eius. Redde eam ad vigiliam.*" As Dagger slipped into the old tongue, I didn't struggle to follow. All witches were taught the tongue of the Mother and Father as children, but it was rarely used. The candles went out, plunging us into darkness. None of us moved until one of the candles flickered back on, just before Xava groaned.

"Thank you," I muttered in prayer. "Xava, are you okay?"

"Where are we?" She asked, her voice husky from lack of use.

"We're at our hotel in Mercy Valley. Just sit up slowly." Alura helped her up, fluffing the pillows so she could sit back comfortably.

"You got got by a Dream witch. We had to perform a spell to bring you out of it." Dagger said.

"Oh... Well, that's embarrassing." She shrugged, "Good job pulling me out of it without a Protection witch."

"How are you calm?" I asked, grinding my teeth, "You've been in a magically induced sleep for hours. Dream witches are known for showing you your worst fears."

I watched as Xava and Dagger shared a meaningful look. "Come sit with me." She said, patting the bed next to her. Alura had already moved the candles, leaving us free to sit around her. "Markus, I have been a member of the Hex Guard most of my life. Enduring pain and torture was an early part of my training. I'm fine."

"What were you shown?" Dagger asked before I could respond.

"Mostly the night that Garith eradicated the Dovey Coven on loop." She responded as if that was a perfectly normal thing to endure over and over again.

I jerked away from her in horror as Dagger cursed, "That means he knows where you're going."

"Maybe." She responded, "Let him come. I think there is business that needs to be finished."

"He's a commander in the Hex Guard. Are you crazy?" I stood, pacing beside the bed. "You can't seriously think we're going to fight him."

"No… I'm going to kill him the same way he's killed my family and hundreds of other witches and warlocks. The Mother and Father have blessed us; I can prove that to the council." Xava explained.

"You won't win that battle. Not if you kill Garith." Dagger said, gravely.

"I will. I have to. And those visions have given me an idea." She brushed him off, crawling toward the end of the bed to stand.

"No," I said, my voice echoing through the room as my magic responded to my emotions. "You will not do anything to put yourself in danger. We can go to this council together with evidence that the accusations against me are lies. I can reach out to some loyal friends, have them act as character witnesses."

"Oh boy," Dagger muttered.

Xava sighed heavily, "Markus, I understand that you're trying to be protective, but leave that to the protection witch."

I saw red at her words. I couldn't stop myself from reaching out and gripping her arm. Before I could think, my hand was wrapped around her throat, "You will listen to me."

Her pupils dilated, the light brown disappearing into black. I could smell her arousal as I squeezed her delicate neck. I felt tension ease out of her body as she fell under the spell of my gaze. I wanted to order her to tell me her plans, wanted to force her to follow the rules that I designed to keep her safe. Clearly, no one had been keeping my girl safe in a very long time. Instead, I made a split-second decision, "Strip out of your clothes." I released her, waiting, almost hoping that she would disobey me. She didn't even hesitate to rip her shirt over her head, pushing her pants and panties down in one go. When she stood before me naked, I circled her, taking a moment to visually inspect her body. I loved her ass most, the large pale globs jiggled slightly when I couldn't stop myself from slapping them. Her breasts hung heavily, nipples hard in the cool room. I traced my hands over her belly; I loved the softness and curves of her body. It was so different from my own hardness. "Your safeword is grinch. If at any time you need us to stop, you'll say that. Say it now so I know that you understand."

Her nose scrunched up slightly as she said, "Grinch." It was ridiculous, but I knew there was no doubt that we'd know if she needed us to stop.

"Good girl. Tonight, your bonds are going to push your limits. First, I want you on your knees." She sank to the floor at my command.

Alura appeared, red silk rope hanging from her hand, "You want the pleasure, or should I?"

"You're better at it." I conceded, motioning for her to tie Xava to her liking. I took a seat on the couch in the center of the room, watching as Alura ran her fingers over Xava's breasts, pinching at her nipples before beginning the tie I'd seen her do only once before.

Dagger took a seat next to me, watching as well, "So I was right?" He muttered. The comment made me want to punch him, but the sight of Xava's breasts being tied in rope was more important than his cockiness. Alura worked with a focus I couldn't imagine having, tying and twisting that long piece of rope in an artful way that left Xava at our mercy. Her hands were tied behind her back, pushing her breasts even further forward. The rope around her legs kept them open, giving us a beautiful glimpse of her pussy, the small trail of red curls like an arrow to what I wanted most. Dagger groaned from beside me, "I think we're going to learn to get along just fine. Want to clue me in on the plan for her?"

"Just do what I say," I growled, standing when Alura nodded to me. Xava stared up at me as I bent down to look her in the eyes, "We are going to push your limits tonight. All of us are going to wring pleasure from you until you're begging for it to stop, but there will be pain as well. Do you understand?" She nodded, and I reached out, slapping my hand right over her nipple. She pitched forward, but I grabbed the rope at her back to steady her, "When you are asked a question, you will respond 'yes or no, sir.'" Alura coughed, and I added, "Or ma'am."

"Yes sir." Her voice was soft, and I noticed the look in her eyes. Xava was meant to be a submissive. I looked forward to seeing her dominant side, but she was already slipping into sub space so easily.

I reached into the open bag that Alura had dropped on the bed, grabbing a blind fold. "Tonight you won't know which of us is touching you." I slipped it over her head, settling it over her eyes. I motioned for Dagger, handing him two items from the bag. His eyes widened before a grin spread across his face. Together, we maneuvered Xava onto the bed. I tucked a pillow under her hips to make sure she stayed comfortable as we played with her. Vibrating filled the room as Alura pulled out a wand. She climbed behind Xava, pressing her lips against her spine just before she slipped the wand between her legs. Xava tried to move, but restrained, she couldn't escape the vibrations. I watched as Alura grabbed a smaller piece of rope, carefully tying the wand in place. I grinned at her as she moved away. All three of us stood and watched as Xava was forced into her first orgasm, her screams muffled by the bed as the wand relentlessly vibrated. As she shook and squirmed from the first orgasm, Dagger drew back the flogger I'd handed him.

Xava jumped, crying out as the braided rope made contact with her ass. I watched as he laid into her over and over, occasionally dragging the flogger over her dripping pussy. When her ass was covered in red strips, I stepped in, grabbing another toy from the bag. Dagger got on the other side of me as we both inserted a toy into each of her holes. Her cries as we stuffed her full were music to my ears. My cock was weeping in my pants, but I wasn't ready to take her yet. Watching as Dagger played with the butt plug he'd shoved into her ass made me imagine the two of us taking her at the same time. It wouldn't be tonight, she wasn't nearly ready for that, but soon. The small vibrating egg I'd slipped inside her pussy was coated with my magic, and I watched an evil sort of glee as she was pushed into a second and third orgasm back to back. Her swollen red ass bounced as she moved, trying desperately to get away from the pleasure we were forcing onto her. Alura appeared between us, tossing the wand away, and lapping at Xava's swollen, dripping pussy. Her mews had gotten more pathetic, and I pulled her up, helping her sit on Alura's face. The blindfold was soaked in her tears, so I pulled it away, grabbing her chin so she could look at me. "If you're a good girl and come all over Alura's face, Dagger will take your pussy while I take your mouth." I couldn't help myself as I bent my head, pulling one of her hard nipples into my mouth. I groaned at the taste of her skin, nipping slightly before I moved to the next one. It wasn't long before she was screaming again as Alura forced another orgasm out of her. Her body spasmed in my arms, unable to take the pleasure any longer. I sat back, easing her into my lap.

I was shocked when she looked up at me, "May I please have your cock."

"Goddamn, Xav, you're so fucking hot." I groaned, fumbling to get my cock free of my pants. As soon as it sprang free, she licked the pre-cum from my tip, causing my eyes to roll back in my head. She sucked my cock with a vigor that I'd never experienced before. I was embarrassed by how quickly she brought me to the edge. I gripped her hair, stopping her movements as I motioned for Dagger to take his position. As soon as he pushed inside her, she was back on my cock, the tip bumping the back of her throat.

"I've been dreaming of this for years," Dagger said, as he slammed into her with a viciousness that I appreciated. She screamed around my cock, and I was unsurprised to see that Alura had gotten the wand and was pushing Xava into another orgasm. Dagger followed her, male moans filling the room as I nearly came as well.

I saw stars when Xava's entire body seized with a final orgasm. I spilled my seed down her throat. Forcing her to swallow it as she shook and cried from the pleasure. Bruises had appeared on her hips where Daggers' fingers had been. Alura rushed to untie Xava as she gasped and shook from the sheer amount of pleasure, we'd subjected her to.

"Shh, you did so good, red. Came so many times for us." She murmured, tossing the rope away, and she pulled Xava to her chest. Dagger and I moved mindlessly toward the bed, climbing in on either side of the women. Our bodies stayed that way, slick with sweat and juices as we all drifted off to sleep.

# *Seven*

*Xava*

Watching Markus huff and puff as we hiked up the trail that led to my family's property shouldn't have made me laugh. Alura wasn't much better off; her cheeks were bright red as she jogged up to me, "Are we getting close? I don't want to have to carry Markus' fat ass up the rest of the way."

I snorted, "Yes, one more curve and we'll be there."

We walked in silence for a moment before she said, "I'm sorry about all of this."

I glanced at her, taking in her stunning features, barely comprehending what she said, "Sorry for what?"

"It seems like Markus and I have caused you far more problems than we're worth," Alura said, refusing to meet my eyes.

I stopped in my tracks, glancing back to see that Markus and Dagger were far behind us. "Alura, I wouldn't trade the time we've gotten together for the world. The last few days have probably been the best time I've had since I was a child. It's more my fault than yours that we're in this mess."

Her steel blue eyes finally met mine, and the tears there took my breath away. "It makes me angry that these are the best days you've ever had. I'd like to rip whatever asshole hurt you into tiny little shreds."

"Don't you dare put yourself in any danger for me. I'm very good at protecting myself." I said. The image of Alura trying to fight Garith filled me with horror. She was no match for his power.

Markus and Dagger caught up with us before she could respond, but I caught the glimpse of fire in her eyes that made my heart stop. We walked in silence until I felt magic start to curl around my ankles, a long-dormant spell keyed to my blood reacting. The Earth shook slightly as we passed through the barrier that should have protected my coven from the Hex Guard so long ago. To this day, I didn't know how they'd gotten through the protection spell. I'd considered many possibilities over the years, but ultimately, I doubt I'd ever know. "Everyone hold hands," I shouted before they stepped through. Alura's warm hand grabbed mine, and we all stumbled into the circle of small cabins I'd been raised in. My stomach turned at the bleached bones that had been undisturbed for almost twenty years. Twenty years that I'd been a member of the Hex Guard, trained to end the lives of my fellow witches. My parents would be sick if they could see me today.

"I will take care of them," Dagger said, stepping forward. I watched with my Other sight as the grey of his magic wrapped around the bones that were scattered everywhere. He whispered, "Mother and Father allow to lay the former Dovey coven to rest. Pax in morte." Slowly, the bones turned to ash, floating away in a wind that was anything but natural. Tears filled my eyes against my will as I realized that my family had never been given a proper burial.

Markus wrapped an arm around my shoulder, "Take the time that you need. We'll clean up one of these cabins so that we have a place to rest."

I nodded and found myself wandering off into the woods. I trusted them to handle choosing a place for us to rest without me.

It was odd to trust someone for the first time since I was a child. Especially Markus and Alura, while I'd been stalking Markus for months, I still barely knew them. Yet something about them was right. Dagger wasn't surprising if I allowed myself to think about it. I'd had feelings for him long before I insisted to start working alone, but feelings were nothing but a danger in the Hex Guard. It was against the Code to sleep with your mission partners.

I was so lost in my thoughts that I didn't notice the root sticking up in the path I was walking on until it was too late. I tumbled forward, my knees hitting the ground hard, my ankle twisting as it got stuck in the root. I grunted, rolling over onto my butt as pain shot up my leg. "Son of a bitch." I groaned.

I sat there for a long moment, as my leg throbbed, and my boot became impossible to keep on. I bit my cheek as I yanked it off, pulling the thick sock with it. I was trained to ignore pain, so once the immediate throbbing stopped, I stood, walking gingerly back toward the center of camp. A tear rolled down my cheek unchecked. I glanced down, noticing that my foot was turning purple.

"Xava, why are you carrying your--" Markus stopped speaking, rushing toward me as I started to pitch forward. I felt magic wrap around me before I could hit the ground. I turned my head, noticing Dagger running toward me.

"What happened?" He asked in a panic.

"I just tripped. It's fine." I responded, ignoring the way my vision swam.

"Your foot is fucking broken." Markus snapped.

My heart was beating too fast, I knew that, but there was nothing I could do as I blacked out from the pain.

*Alura*

Xava was lying on the bed I'd managed to clean up before she returned. She was asleep as Dagger and Markus whispered to one another about what to do. Her ankle was broken, of that I was certain. It hung at an odd angle as I inspected it, purple and blue bruising already spreading up her leg.

"We can't call someone to heal it, and I know I can't mess with life magic," Dagger grunted as his eyes took in the damage.

"Well, we can't just leave her like that! What if somebody shows up looking for us? She won't be able to protect herself properly." Markus ran his fingers through his hair as he paced beside the bed.

"I'll try," I said, standing up.

Markus stopped, meeting my eyes, "I don't know if that's a good idea."

He knew the truth that I wouldn't speak in front of anyone else. My magic was weak at best. I'd gotten a bit of a boost when Markus and I had bonded. Each time we'd performed a spell together, my magic stretched and struggled inside me to keep up with his power. When the bond with Xava and Dagger snapped into place, I felt a boost, but I hadn't truly used my power since that happened. It was time to find out if I could hang with these powerful warlocks surrounding me. "I have to."

Dagger and Markus moved to one side of the room as I crawled onto the bed. I folded my legs underneath me, placing my palms on my knees. I took a deep breath and reached for the magic that had disappointed me time and time again. It was sluggish as it responded to my request. Once I felt it starting to swirl in my chest, I began to speak, "Father, I call upon you today. Grant me the power to heal the wound of my bond." I closed my eyes, forcing my magic into my hands as I moved them to Xava's leg. Nothing happened for several beats, my magic grinding to a halt inside me. I growled in frustration, "Mother, grant me your blessing." Heat filled my hands, causing me to open my eyes. Purple and golden light wrapped around my fingers. I almost panicked seeing the color of the Mother and Father on my hands, but I forced myself to focus on my intention. I watched in shock as the bruises on her foot slowly disappeared. The magic faded as suddenly as it had come on, leaving me dizzy.

Xava's eyelashes fluttered before revealing her perfect honey brown eyes filled with confusion. "Why do I keep waking up feeling like I've missed something?"

"Because you keep having bad shit happen to you," Dagger responded casually. "The broken foot can't be blamed on the Hex Guard, though. That was just Xava's usual clumsiness."

"I am not clumsy." She insisted, sitting up. I couldn't help myself, I leaned forward, pressing my lips to hers before she could say anything else. I hadn't felt this strongly for anyone before. I'd known I was different when I was a kid, as the other little girls started to get interested in boys, I found myself interested in my friends. Of course, being a witch made it easier when I came out. My parents had no problem with my sexuality; all sex witches were at least a little fluid. The fact that I'd ended up bonded to a man had been a source of stress for them. They knew our joining would be difficult for me, but no witch dared to deny the blessed bond of the Mother and Father. "I love you," Xava muttered as I pulled away. We both stared at each other, the shock in her eyes told me she didn't intend to say those words.

I grinned, "I love you too, red."

"I have the urge to yell gay so badly right now." Dagger chuckled from the corner.

I rolled my eyes, "Very mature."

I stood, "We need food. I'm going to go work on a fire. Why don't you big, strong men go hunt?"

Markus and Dagger filed out the door without another word. Xava climbed off the bed, an odd look in her eyes as she glanced around the dusty cabin we stood in. I could almost see the memories playing behind her eyes; the pain there made my heart ache for her. I couldn't imagine what she had been through at such a young age. My childhood had been peaceful and happy in a way that was very rare. Maybe the Mother blessed me with a peaceful childhood so I could help Xava through her struggles, show her a different side of life. Maybe one day we would have a child... My eyes widened at my own thoughts. Having a child wasn't something I'd ever considered before, but as I watched Xava pick through drawers, quiet sighs leaving her full lips, I couldn't help but smile at the idea of her carrying a child on her hip. A little girl with her bright red hair and Markus' green eyes filled my mind's eyes, bringing a tear to my eye. I did love Markus, just not in the way that would have made our bond easier.

"Weren't you going to build a fire?" Xava asked, a hand on her hip and a twinkle in her eye as she stared me down.

"I'm a witch, baby, I can whip up a fire with the snap of my fingers," I said, my voice dropping an octave as I moved toward her.

Her eyebrow raised, "I bet you I can whip up something even better." The look in her eyes had my body heating up with arousal. Xava may be soft and submissive most of the time, but right now, I could see the steel in her. Years of being trained by the Hex Guard gave her an edge that was completely unexpected at first glance. Xava didn't hesitate to grab my face and pull me down to her mouth. This kiss was different from before, fiery in a way I wasn't prepared for. Somehow, she grabbed my ponytail, yanking me down until I was on my knees before her. "I like you like this." She muttered.

"You can have me anyway you want me." I breathed, desperate for her control. Those words were all she needed; with a snap of her fingers, all of our clothes disappeared. She was a strong witch, of course, she had to be, considering her line of work, but I was still impressed. From my angle, I had the perfect look at her pussy, the curve of her belly accentuated her sexiness, making her perfectly soft. In my mind, the Mother probably looked much the same. Soft and supple with a core of steel. I wanted to worship at Xava's feet for eternity. "May I taste you?" I asked.

She sat on the bed and spread her legs wide for me, "Crawl to me, Lura." Her husky voice commanded me. I did as she asked without a second thought, crawling between her legs until I was pressing kisses into her thighs. "Don't tease me." She demanded, shifting her hips closer to my face. I dove into her with the desperation of a starving man, lapping slowly at first. When she moved her hips faster, begging for me, I indulged her desire, working her into a frenzy faster than I could have expected. When her thighs started to shake, and her fingers dug into my skull, I knew she was close. I sucked her clit into my mouth, humming slightly until she came undone with a shout. I stayed between her legs, waiting until the aftershocks had subsided completely, before I went to do it again. This time, she stopped me, grabbing me by my hair and sitting up. "It's my turn to have some fun with you. Get on the bed." I scrambled to follow her directions, not stopping the moans that fell from my mouth as she ran her hands down my body. Her fingers were gentle at first, softly caressing my breasts, brushing down my stomach. When her hand cupped my pussy, I grinded into her palm. Desperate for her to do something. She grinned, and I watched golden magic coalesce in her other hand until a shiny dildo was held aloft. "I'm going to fuck every one of your holes with this." My eyes widened. No one had ever taken all of me the way she wanted to, but I couldn't deny her. "Are you going to be a good girl for me, Alura?"

"Anything for you, Xava," I responded.

She didn't disappoint me. Slowly, she drove me wild, sitting on my face as she slammed the dildo deep into my pussy. We came in unison that time. When she climbed off of me, I had some hope that she'd forgotten her earlier threat, but she had me flipped onto my stomach in seconds, her warm fingers running over my hole. She continued to fuck my pussy with the dildo, driving me closer to a second orgasm, but just before I was about to finish again, she pulled it out, pressing it into my ass relentlessly. I gasped and groaned, but she pressed on until she had every inch inside me. I wasn't prepared when her warm mouth sucked on my clit as she fucked my ass harder and harder with the dildo. That orgasm snuck up on me, a scream ripping from my throat without a thought for the men who had disappeared earlier.

Finally, she relented, pulling my longer body into her lap to cuddle on the bed. We lay in silence for a long time, until she finally said, "I think this is what I always wanted."

"You have me until the Mother and Father call me home," I responded, kissing her tummy, and then her chest, and eventually her lips. Our bodies tangled in each other until we fell asleep, our bodies exhausted from pleasure.

# Eight



*Xava*

Fresh mountain air was the best thing for the soul. I knew that without a doubt as I sat on a rock watching as the sun rose over the Smokies. The amazing sex I'd had with Alura the night before didn't hurt either. I'd awoken to find Markus had crawled into bed with us. I was always up early; five in the morning was the expected time for anyone in the Hex Guard to start their day. I knew Dagger was somewhere nearby; I could sense his magic in the air, but I had decided to leave him to his business. When the sun was high in the sky, I stood, stretching and deciding to head back to the cabins. Today, I would put my own protections in place around the ward the Doveys had built.

There was a chill in the air, as was normal for February, but something about it raised the hair on my arms. I walked slowly, straining my ears to hear anything that would set off alarm bells. As I walked, I started to think, and with a gasp, I realized today was Valentine's Day. The day was sacred to witches because it was said that the Mother and Father's bond had solidified on this day thousands of years ago. It's the day that Markus and Alura were supposed to join before the Black Coven. My chest tightened; they would never be forced to join again now. I would find a way to make all of this right.

When I stepped into the clearing, Markus was standing outside the cabin, a look of guilt on his face. As I approached, he sighed, "Good, I was afraid you'd been kidnapped."

"What's wrong?" I asked, ignoring his comment.

He sighed, "You're very perceptive."

I raised an eyebrow, waiting for him to respond to my question. My face paled when he pulled a cell phone from his pocket. "What did you do?"

"I just called Fang. I needed eyes on the--"

"You fucking idiot." Alura snapped, stepping out of the cabin, "Fang isn't even part of our coven anymore!"

"He's my best friend. He'd never do anything to harm me." Markus argued.

"Until he remembers how you tricked him into joining the Black Coven." She snapped again, "How stupid can you be?"

"You're not the least bit curious what he told me?" Markus said, refusing to deflate under her anger.

We both stared at him in silence, waiting for him to tell us something. "Fang and Bambi visited the coven. Take a wild guess who is leading while we're away."

"Vince." Alura said, "We already knew--"

"Let me finish." He said, "Fang did a little digging. He found a broken spell; he thinks he has proof that Vince directly communicated with someone in the Hex Guard."

"He did." The voice that was spoken had my blood freezing in my body. I turned slowly, barely breathing as Garith came into view. His bald head shone under the bright morning sun. I felt Markus stiffen, but I held my hand up, forcing him to stay in place. "I hate to say it, Xava, but you've disappointed me. You should have known that I'd expect you to come here."

I had considered that, but I had calculated that we would have time to prepare for him. "Seems like I've been a disappointment most of my life."

Garith curled his lip, "I smell the cannibal around here somewhere, too. Two of my assassins betraying me in the same week has not put me in a good mood."

"How have I betrayed you exactly?" I asked, trying to buy time to come up with a plan. I needed to know exactly what he already knew.

"Disobeying direct orders, leaving a mission without completion, entering a forbidden area... Really, Xava, I could go on. I didn't raise you to behave like this." He didn't move, but the tension in his body had me preparing for a fight. I wasn't certain that I could win. Garith had trained me; he knew all of the tricks I'd learned over the last twenty years. If he'd managed to track me here, then there was no doubt in my mind he was prepared to end my life today. "I wish I could say I'm surprised, but that filthy Dovey blood has always been strong in your veins."

Rage flared in me, years of his degrading my heritage flashed through my mind faster than I could process. I didn't realize I was moving until a golden blade formed in my hand. Shouts went up all around me as I swung that blade at the man who had raised me, trained me. He'd made me this monster; we would see how he enjoyed playing with it.  Of course, my blade didn't land. His harsh laugh echoed in my ears, and my arms jolted from the force of my blade meeting his shield. A dance began, him defending, me attacking until sweat ran down my back. "Giving up already? That's unlike you, Xava." He taunted as I stepped back, assessing the situation, letting oxygen fill my lungs.

A sudden realization settled over me. I glanced to where Markus and Alura stood, the look of agony on their faces as they watched me fight was enough to instantly cool my rage. I had a family again, and this time I wouldn't fail them. I wouldn't become the monster Garith wanted me to be.

I let the sword dissipate from my hand, "Fighting you gains me nothing, because you are nothing."

I turned my back on him in the greatest act of disrespect I could think of. I only made it a few steps before agony ripped through me. The blade plunged through my chest, and the gasps of horror from the people I loved were my final moments before the world went black around me.

### Dagger

I bit my tongue to keep silent as Xava dropped to her knees. A sword I'd become intimately familiar with at the hands of Garith plunged directly through the center of her chest. My magic swirled in my hands, begging to be unleashed, to rip the soul from the man who had taken *everything* from me. Only the movement from Markus stopped me. Bright pink magic flared around him as his own grief and rage consumed him. Alura didn't move to stop him as he rushed toward Garith. It was the perfect distraction for me.

I moved in silence and shadow to Xava's body. Death was more comforting to me than life, but seeing the glazed look in her eyes was enough to nearly bring me to my knees. I could see her perfect golden soul floating just above her body, desperately trying to cling to the life that had been so cruelly ripped away from her. I willed my magic to wrap around it, grey dimming the golden light as I slowly yanked it toward me. I breathed deeply, fighting the discomfort as I made a place in my own body for her soul. The warmth that filled me as it entered my chest was pleasant, not the burning sensation I was expecting, as if her soul was already a part of me. I prayed to the Father, begging for time as I continued to move, shrouding her body in magic so that it could not be harmed any further.

My next stop was Alura's side. She had collapsed from the ground, eerie wails leaving her throat as she watched Markus fight Garith. He wasn't winning by any means, his body covered in long slashes, but he was still holding his own. I hated to admit it, but the pretty boy had impressed me. "Get up," I commanded her.

Her blue eyes met mine, her sadness replaced with rage, "Where were you? Why didn't you stop this?"

"I could not." That was the only answer I gave. Xava would have prevented any of us from stepping in. She had a score to settle with Garith, and my interference would not have been welcomed, "But if you help me, I can fix this."

"How?" She said, a bit of hope filling her eyes.

"I need magic," I said.

Her face deflated, "I don't have much power."

I furrowed my eyebrows, "You healed her. You were the Priestess of the Black Coven."

"And it is my greatest shame to have not been blessed by the Mother and Father." She snapped, her rage returning, "You'll need Markus."

"No," I growled, "It will be you. Whatever magic you have will have to do."

She sighed, but nodded. I grabbed her hand, moving us silently until we were behind Garith. From my pockets, I produced the obsidian I had spent the morning searching for. It wasn't often a warlock needed this kind of focus, but I prayed it would work. I sat on the ground, erecting a small shield around us so that Garith could not see what I planned to do. "Summon whatever magic you can." I instructed Alura, "Keep your intentions pure and focused on Xava. Her red hair, those big brown eyes..." I trailed off as her smiling face appeared in my mind's eye. Alura's hands started to glow a pale pink, flickering, but fighting, "You can do this. For her."

"Anything for Xava." She growled, closing her eyes. The magic glowed, and I set the large rock in her palm, laying my own hand over the top.

"Do not fear. Do not listen. Do not lose focus." I commanded before I began to chant. The words were nonsense to anyone but the spirits I called on. My magic was fire under my skin as I dove past the veil, seeking my targets. In my mind, the world morphed, blooming and beautiful in a way that was unexpected. Finally, a clearing, so clearly a replica of the one we sat in, formed. Two figures appeared, floating toward me. As they solidified, I knew they were the people I sought, "I am Dagger Damascus Ladron. Your daughter's soul lives in me. I come to seek your help."

"We know who ya are, boy. We have watched our Xava grow." Xava's father was a huge man; even his soul had a commanding presence. "You seek something that is not natural."

"Is it natural what was done to you? Is it natural what was done to her... to me? Do you not seek vengeance on the man who harmed her?" I shot back in desperation.

"Revenge will not bring peace." Xava's mother shared her fiery red hair and curvy body, "It is not the way of the Mother to seek revenge."

"So you will do nothing?" I asked. The world around me flickered, and I knew I was running out of time, "Xava's bonded still live, I still live. She hasn't given up yet, but you know it won't be long."

"There is a way." Her father said, glancing down at his wife, "Only rumors, but… The Dovey will stand behind you."

I breathed a sigh of relief, "That is all I need."

"Son… If it works, you will all be changed." Her mother warned, her voice far away as the veil began to fade from my mind, "There is always a price to pay."

"I will pay any price for Xava, my soul if that's what they require," I responded.

When I opened my eyes, Alura's face was pale, "Did it work?"

I took a deep breath, feeling something new blooming inside of me, "I think so, but we need to get to Markus. Now."

We both stood, dispelling the magic we had worked. Alura wobbled on her feet for a moment, but stabilized quickly, rushing toward Garith and Markus who were still locked in battle. As soon as we were close enough, I threw out a spell, stunning Garith long enough for Markus to rush to us. "What's going on?"

"I need you to trust me." I responded, "Join hands."

He didn't even hesitate, grabbing mine and Alura's hands in seconds. "Mother, Father, you know what I seek. You see the evil that has been done here in your name. Please accept our sacrifice as payment, please allow us to protect our bonded and this land from any further suffering." I prayed aloud before I began the spell, "Whatever magic you have left, pull it to the surface." I commanded them. "Death falls to its knees before you, Sex has no place without you. Mother, you provided us life, Father, you provided us love. Accept the return of our power to bring back the one that you chose for us." I felt Markus' hand tighten, but he did as I asked, pink and grey magic swirled between us. For a heart-stopping moment I feared that the spell had failed, but purple light flashed from the sky, acting as a vacuum until the last of our power disappeared.

My head was foggy as the spell came to an end. Alura and Markus were pale and shaking as Garith approached us. An odd look of glee on his face, "You really tried to sacrifice you're worthless magic for her life? I had no idea the cannibal was such a sappy lover."

Those words were the last thing I heard before I passed out from sheer exhaustion.

# Nine

Xava

I was in a strange place. I didn't quite recognize the trees that surrounded me, but it still felt like home. I floated above the ground rather than walking, as I moved slowly, the scenery became more and more familiar. Finally, I came to a waterfall, a flash of memory nearly causing me to collapse to the ground. A beautiful summer day, splashing around in the small pond, eating a gooey sandwich tucked behind the waterfall with my mother. It was so joyous that my eyes filled with tears. I hadn't felt that much happiness since then.

"My little cherry pie, you've grown up so much since then." The soft voice of my mother would always be familiar to my ears.

I spun around, taking in her round face, so much like my own, "Momma?"

"Come, you have so many people who want to see you today." Her hand wrapped around mine, calloused and warm.

Something in the back of my mind fluttered, but I ignored it, allowing my mother's grey form to lead me toward... home. I knew it the moment we stepped into the clearing. Some of my cousins, unchanged by the many years that had passed, ran through the meadow we'd grown up in. Every Dovey was here, with big smiles on their faces and bear hugs as they noticed me.

"Let me have my daughter," My father's voice boomed, cutting the crowd that had formed around me. His strong arms wrapped around my body, warmth bleeding from him into me. "My Xava." He breathed, "You've grown so much." He pulled away, holding my shoulder as he looked me up and down, "Pretty like your mama, but you're strong like me. I'm so proud of you. You are the very best parts of us."

A sob escaped my throat, and I let myself fall back into his arms. Years of emotional torment from watching my loved ones die filled me. My family pressed in all around us, a hum coming from them. The Dovey Coven had always been full of love, and in that moment, I saw every bit of it flood into me. It healed the grief and pain I'd suffered for years as I came to understand beyond a shadow of a doubt that their sacrifice had been freely given. None of them blamed me for surviving; in fact, they were proud to see the woman I had become. I had done well in the Hex Guard, even if Garith had poisoned most of my life.

I gasped, pulling away, "What happened to Markus, Alura, and Dagger. I need to get back up."

My father opened his mouth to respond, but a bright purple light flashed through the greyness of our world. Two figures appeared in the center of the clearing, their bodies covered in shadows, the darkest black I'd ever seen. I watched as all of my family fell to their knees around me. Only then did it hit me that the Mother and Father were appearing before my very eyes.

"Child, time is of the essence. We have given you this moment with your family out of kindness. A great wrong was done against the Dovey Coven twenty years ago. It is time that you make it right." The Mother's voice rolled over me like a song, raising the hair on the back of my neck.

"I don't understand," I said, moving toward them against my will.

"Your bonds have performed a ritual unlike any other before. They have sacrificed our gifts to give you life again. Time passes *differently here, but you have only moments to make a decision. Will you rejoin them or stay here with your family?" The Father's voice was like iron as it clapped around me.*

*"They didn't." I gasped, "I'm dead." I stated dumbly. My brain processed the information they'd given me quicker than I could react. I glanced back to find that only my parents remained. I rushed back to them, throwing myself into their arms. "I have to go back."*

*"We know." Mama said, smoothing my hair down, "It is not time for you to join us yet."*

*"Keep them in line, Xava. And keep doing the Dovey name proud. Rebuild what we once were." Daddy said, pressing his lips to the top of my head, "We will be reunited when your journey ends."*

*I turned back to the Mother and Father, "What will this cost them? I can't have bonds with no magic."*

*"Have faith in us, daughter. It is time to return." The Mother said, a ghostly white hand extending to touch my chest.*

I came awake with a gasp, the bright sunlight and cold air a shock to my body, I wasn't prepared for. I heard voices behind me, and I scrambled to my feet. Yanking the blade that was still lodged in my healed chest out, magic dripping from it as I held it aloft. I took in the scene; only Alura still stood. Blood dripped from her mouth as she swung her fist at Garith. His movements were lazy, taunting her into a fight that was sure to kill her. Dagger and Markus were collapsed on either side of her. With a preternatural silence, I moved, my blade cutting through Garith's wrist before he could land the punch on Alura. With a sick thump, his hand fell to the ground. I found pain and panic in his eyes as I moved my body between him and Alura. My magic was strong as I called for another blade.

"How?" He stuttered as I stepped toward him.

"Something you can't ever begin to comprehend…" I trailed off, lifting my blades, preparing to kill the man who had murdered my entire family, "Love."

His jaw hung open, moments from a response, as I sliced one blade through his neck and the other through his waist. Blood sprayed all over me, my magic flaring around me as I turned, kicking the pieces of him across the meadow. I was panting, both blades in my hands as I turned back toward Alura.

Her blonde and black hair was tangled around her pale face as she took me in. Markus and Dagger were both sitting up, dazed and barely moving, as I dropped the blades to the ground. I rushed toward them, magic already worked to heal their wounds.

Dagger coughed, "That may haunt my wet dreams for the rest of my days."

"New kink unlocked." Markus joked back, groaning as he stood.

Alura was the first one to wrap their arms around me, but it wasn't long before all four of us sat in the dirt, gripping one another. I pulled away, touching all of them as much as I could, ensuring to myself that they were real and alive, "You gave up your powers."

"I would choose you over anything in any life," Markus said, grabbing my face. "There was never a moment of doubt."

My mind blanked out, an image appearing to me. "I can fix it," I said suddenly.

"We chose this, Xava. So long as we get to stay with you, our magic doesn't matter." Dagger said, trying to stop me from standing.

"Hush," I said, waving him off as I rushed into the closest cabin. I pulled out pristine, white linen clothing and six black candles. I shouldn't have known that they'd be there, much less still in perfect condition, but nothing mattered but the task the Mother and Father had shown me. "Change," I instructed them as I rushed around our small circle, placing and lighting each candle in a careful pattern. I watched as they stripped naked, donning the simple white clothing without complaint. I did the same, forcing myself not to blush as all of their eyes took in my body. I stepped into the center of the circle, "Join hands around me." I summoned all of my magic into my chest, "With the blessing of the Dovey, I call on the Mother and Father. Grant us this chance to prove ourselves as the new Priests of the new Dovey Coven." I forced myself to ignore the way that Alura's eyes widened. The flames on the candles grew taller, "On this, the Day of Joining, judge our souls, Mother and Father. See our flaws and know that we will work each day toward your goals." A quiet hum filled the meadow, and I watched Dagger stiffen. Only he could sense the spirits that crossed over the veil, "See that we have the support of my ancestors. Allow us to be the new protectors of these mountains, where the Mother and Father once walked." The words that came from my mouth were a surprise to me, but the flames on the candle blew out. A purple orb danced in the sky above us. Bright golden light flashed next, and suddenly I was forced to the ground. I watched as that golden light filled Markus, then Dagger, and finally Alura. I counted the seconds, my breathing uneven as slowly the colors faded. Dagger raised his hand, a golden light dancing along his fingers as he summoned a dagger. I'd seen him do that move a million times, but somehow it was different. Smoother.

"I've never felt this much power." Alura choked, a shield appearing on her arm with ease.

Markus was silent, an odd look on his face as golden light fluttered between his fingers. Our eyes met, and a small grin spread across his face. "We're a coven."

"The Dovey Coven to be exact." I grinned back. He stood, wrapping his arms around me, before he spun me in a circle, causing me to shriek.

A melodic voice filled my ears, *"You will be called upon one day... to pay for the gift we have granted you... Prepare... But remember... The love you share is the greatest gift we have given..."*

From the look in the eyes that all met mine, we'd heard the same message. We'd promised our gods something. Something that we wouldn't know the answer to for some time to come. I felt anxiety well in my chest until Markus squeezed me. No, it was worth any price. The four of us were a coven; together, we would find our way through life.

<h1 style="text-align:center">*Ten*</h1>

S everal months passed in what felt like the blink of an eye. Somehow, evidence of Garith's wrongdoing had been presented to the Hex Guard, exonerating us of any crime we may have committed. Our Coven, while berated for joining without permission, was granted full status, and the Dovey name was cleared after twenty years of shame. Fang and Bambi had been the first visitors to come to our home on the mountain; they brought everything Markus and Alura had left behind. The Blood Priestess had cooed over my bright red hair, joking that maybe her bonded and I were related. The grumpy man did remind me of a cousin I met once as a young child, but I laughed off her bubbly chitchat.

Dagger and I slowly found a new normal. Without missions from the Hex Guard, there was nothing for us to do. We, of course, had been honorably discharged from our duties due to our witch bond. Thankfully, the Dovey property was in desperate need of cleaning and maintenance. I was currently bent over picking freshly ripe blackberries from a bush I'd found about a mile into the deep forest. As I stood, I noticed the silence of the animals, and my skin tingled as I realized I was being watched. I lifted the corner of the light blue milkmaid dress I'd slipped into this morning, stepping into the sunlight more fully.

I screamed as a hand clamped over my mouth, thrashing wildly as I was lifted off my feet. My face was pushed into the hardwood of a tree before I finally recognized the warmth at my back. Dagger pressed himself along my body, his hard cock against my ass, "What a pretty little treat I've come across all alone in the woods."

I stopped myself from smiling before I faked a plea, "Please, don't hurt me."

The shock of steel against my neck caused a thrill to run down my spine. Late one night, I'd reveal this fantasy that had been playing out in my head to Alura. It doesn't surprise me in the least that she shared it with Dagger. This kind of scene was right up his alley.

"Oh, I'm going to hurt you, cherry, but you will enjoy every moment of it." With those words, he began, cutting my beautiful dress away. He stopped for a moment, appreciating that I wore nothing underneath it. A strong hand tangled into my hair, pulling my head back as he brought the knife to my throat again. "I'm going to carve myself into your skin so that you'll never forget me." One of his hands held my breast, rolling my nipple between his fingers as the other held the knife to my back. Markus had tattooed a beautiful, photorealistic rose on my left shoulder blade, so I wasn't surprised to feel the sting of a cut on the right. Something about the knife in my skin caused my pussy to flood with heat, making it hard to stay still as he carved something into my back. All the while, he tortured my breasts, slapping and pulling on them until my eyes were filling with tears.

Finally, the knife dropped to the ground, and both of his hands moved to my hips, spreading my ass cheeks wide as he lined himself up with my entrance. "I'm going to fill your pussy with my cum. You'll have to run home, naked, and dripping." Dagger said just before he plunged into me. He took me with a ferocity that had my screams echoing along the trees. He adjusted, moving two fingers to my clit, playing me like the instrument I was in his hands. As my orgasm washed over me, his fingers clamped around my throat, and I felt the warmth of his seed filling me. I couldn't breathe as we rode our orgasms together. When he released me, I panted, falling to my knees. He lifted me into his arms, careful of my aching shoulder.

He grabbed my full basket of berries before carrying me back to our home. Markus and Alura were sitting on the porch of the largest cabin, chatting casually as Markus whittled another arrow. Dagger walked past them without saying a word, only sitting me down once he'd filled a bathtub with warm water. I sat in the tub while he carefully cleaned my back.

"I want to see it," I said, speaking for the first time since our scene ended.

"Welcome back, cherry. Did that meet your expectations?" Dagger said, pulling out his phone and snapping a photo.

"Yes, even better than I imagined," I admitted, squinting as he turned the camera toward me. I grinned when I saw the shield that he carved into my back, in the center a single bird, a dove I assumed, took flight. "I love it."

He pressed a kiss to my forehead, but before he could speak, the phone in his hands began to ring. He answered, stepping out of my earshot in the hallway. I washed myself quickly, drying off and slipping on a white, fluffy robe before I followed him.

"Yeah... yeah... Everett, I told you where I lost the trail." Dagger sounded frustrated as the gruff voice on the other end of the phone interrupted him. "Listen, I'll send you my location. We're not far from it. I can at least guide you to the spot. Just... be nice to my bonded or else." He hung up the phone, turning and crossing his arms as he looked at me, "You're nosy."

"And you love that about me. So we're going to have a visitor?" I asked.

"In a few days, nothing for you to worry about tonight. Just someone I helped for the Hex Guard." He brushed me off.

"But he's coming here…" I trailed off, raising my eyebrow and waiting for more information.

Dagger sighed, "I'm going to take him to the spot where I lost the trail of his bonded. It's just over the mountain in North Carolina."

"He lost his bond? That's terrible. Well, we will make sure to help him in any way we can." I said, turning on my heel and marching into the kitchen, where Markus was wrapped in a 'kiss the cook' apron. Alura leaned against the counter, popping nuts into her mouth from the bowl he was working on. "We're going to have a visitor in a few days, someone with a lost bond."

"I'll get the guest room ready," Alura said, standing to her full height. She dropped a kiss on my head, "Did you have fun?" She whispered.

I nodded, "Thank you."

With that, we all went about different tasks, quietly preparing dinner and readying a space for Dagger's visitor. The silence in our home was peaceful, never tense or angry. We'd all learned to operate as a single unit. Eventually, we would begin to invite others into our Coven, but for now, I enjoyed the peaceful quiet we'd found together.

Our only goal now was to help other witches and be prepared for the day that we would repay the favor of the Mother and Father.

# Acknowledgements

Thank you for reading Three Little Doves. I love Xava's story, and I am so excited to finally be sharing it with you! I want to start off by acknowledging plus size women everywhere. As a certified fat girl, it has not always been easy moving through our world. I want you to know that you have value, your body is beautiful, and to never ever let anyone convince you otherwise.

Next, as always, I want to thank my husband. Tyler, without you I don't think I'd be half the author I am now.  The love and support you show me everyday keeps me going.

And to my family, the Cantrell Clan, I love you guys so much. Thanks for supporting my dreams.

Finally, to my ARC and street team, my lovely PA's (Leah and Larissa), and every other person who takes the time to support this indie author. It truly means the world to me.

# About the author

Taila Cantrell can be found lurking in the mountains of East Tennessee with her husband. Whether she's at her day job, wrangling the feral blue-collar men, tucked into a local bookstore, or at home curled up with her many cats and two pups, she's always plotting the next story. Her readers can look forward to many genres from fantasy romance to poetry to murder mysteries there is no story Taila isn't willing to give her voice to.

In every story, Taila blends spellbinding romance with trauma, chaos, and hope. Her books remind readers that even in the darkest moments, the heart still remembers how to burn bright.

# Also by

*The Reclaiming Wonderland Series*
Code Red
Code White: Frosted Wonderland
Blue Dreams
Emerald Knights (Coming May 2026)

*The Austral Witches:*
Primal Echoes
One Bloody Night
Two Shadowed Hearts
Three Little Doves
Four Twisted Dreams (Coming March 2026)

*Mercy Valley:*
Wing of the Dragon (Coming April 2026)

*The Tides of Desire Trilogy w/Allena Scott*
A Tide of Secrets and Storms
A Tide of Silver and Sin (coming April 2026)

*Standalones*
Ink and Chaos: A Poetry Collection